# LENOX
# JUSTIFIER OF INNOCENCE
## JANET COLLAZO

**DORRANCE**
PUBLISHING CO
EST. 1920
PITTSBURGH, PENNSYLVANIA 15238

Dorrance Publishing Co
585 Alpha Drive
Pittsburgh, PA 15238
Visit our website at www.dorrancebookstore.com

ISBN: 978-1-6366-1242-3
eISBN: 978-1-6366-1829-6

# PREFACE

Demeter Speaking with Zeuus in the Heavens…In the darkness, there is light…

This world is becoming increasingly dark. Evil seems to be winning, gaining momentum. Over powering all that's good. The scales need to be tipped. Though we cannot interfere with earth and humanity, we cannot idly stand by and watch it be destroyed.

Zeuss: I understand your concern, but you cannot bear a human child. Only one with human blood can save humankind.

Demeter: I know that, so I have thought a long and hard many nights. We can use a human surrogate. I've always wanted another daughter. She will possess your strength and powers, my compassion and empathic abilities within a human form. She will restore the balance of good and evil on earth. Save it from itself, defend those who are innocent, and deliver true justice.

Zeus: This won't be easy; you cannot, we cannot interfere in her upbringing. She needs to live like a normal human girl.

Demeter: I understand, but this has to be done. Someone has to stop what we see happening. The end of humanity and earth as we know it. We must find suitable surrogate parents before it's too late.

Zeus: Very well then, find them, and we will do as you wish.

Demeter: I will begin my search.

She took a big sigh of relief having Zeus on board with her plan.

It was a late Sunday afternoon. Shortly after Josephine's parents pre-mature passing from a tragic car accident. Josephine was out for a walk when she witnessed a man beating a dog.

She put her hand up and yelled at him to stop, when something strange happened. It was as though he was paralyzed by Josephine's hand. He began feeling all the pain he was inflicting on the dog. Josephine felt a surge of power radiating through her body. Though she was not sure what was happening, she kept running towards the man with her hand up, pointing at the man until she could safely take the dog.

The man fell to his knees, begging for her to stop. Conflicted with both anger and sadness, she did not want to stop his pain. Not until he felt and realized all the hurt he caused and promised to change his ways. He passed out from the pain. Josephine then grabbed the dog and brought him to her animal sanctuary. She was in shock and confused by what she just did but determined to find answers.

First priority was to get the dog checked out and treated by the sanctuary vet team. While the dog was being attended to, Josephine pulled Amalia aside to tell her what had happened.

Amalia said, " I think I remember my mom saying something about this. It was something from when you were a kid. She may have some answers or at least know where we could find them." They jumped into Josephine's Jeep and headed to Amalia's house in search of answers. Amalia turned to Josephine and said, "Whatever is happening , it's pretty bad ass."

That must have felt awesome to knock that dude on his ass. They looked at each other and laughed.

Josephine said, "Yes, it felt kinda good but scary. Whatever this is, I want to learn how to control it and why it's happening, so I can use it for good.

"True dat, sista," Amalia replied. ; They both burst into laughter as they headed to see Leskha.

They arrive at auntie Leskha's house and head for some answers. When they walked in, Leskha was waiting for them, eager to learn what had just happened. Josephine explained what happened. Leskha left the room and returned with a scrapbook album. She sat with them both and told Josephine the truth about her parents. She handed her a card for a man named Ogard and told her she needed to seek him out.

"He is a mentor and will have more answers about who you are and what your destiny is. Your parents needed to wait until you were old enough; unfortunately they passed before they could tell you the truth. A week before your mother's passing, she came to me and gave me this. She said that if anything happened to them, to give you this book and card. I was waiting for the right time. Call this man, he will help you learn who you are, teach you how to master your gifts. Teach you all you need to know and train you, so that you can protect yourself and fulfill your destiny. I wish I knew more, but your mother was very vague with me and swore me to secrecy."

With her head spinning from the information she just learned.

Josephine took the card and scrapbook and headed back to the sanctuary. She went in to see how the dog was doing. He was a bit traumatized but perked up and started wagging his tail when she walked into the room.

The vet said he was lucky that he only sustained some bumps and bruises but was going to keep him under observation and clean him up. Josephine settled the dog down and fed him. Afterwards, she went to her office to check on a few things. She pulled out the card and decided to give him a call. Her heart raced and felt hot in the face. She took a deep breath and dialed. He had a soft, kind voice. She introduced herself; he responded he was waiting for her call.

"You can call me Ogard. Come tomorrow morning around ten, and dress comfortably.

The next morning, Josephine heads out to meet Ogard. He lived in a very secluded area, lots of land and forest. She walks up to the house, and a man in his late forties comes out. He's a handsome, distinguished -looking man with a bodybuilder physique. Not at all what she expected.

"You look different than I pictured," she said.

Ogard responded, "Oh yeah, how so?"

"Well, honestly I was expecting you to look like Yoda." They laughed and headed into the house.

Ogard offered Josephine a drink and began to explain things to Josephine.

Ogard: We were waiting till you matured, and for the right time to tell you about your destiny. You have great power, and it's my duty to show you how to maximize and control it. To teach you how to defend yourself. You are destined to defend those who cannot, defend themselves to give a voice to those who can't be heard. The innocent. With each mission, you will make the world a better place and eventually save humanity. It will not be easy, and you will want to give up at times. But be patient, you will become stronger, more vigilant. Don't try to understand everything now. It will come, in time you will get all the answers about who you are, why you're destined. For now let's begin your training.

Josephine: Okay, I'll try, but I'm very confused and somewhat conflicted.

Ogard: "Just trust the process, trust that your parents after their passing are guiding you."

Josephine is in excellent shape. She lifts weights, runs, rock climbs, and jumps rope. So she is looking forward to her training. Ogard explained that this will be a small portion of her learning. He's going to teach her how to meditate, to tap her mind's potential, so she can learn how to harness her powers. She will learn fighting skills, shooting, how to use knives and rope. Essentials for survival.

Josephine admits that meditation is difficult for her; her mind is always going.

"We will start two things. Meditation and fighting style. I will teach you Krav Maga, military -style combat techniques and self -defense. You already have self-discipline and strength, we just need to hone down your skills. Teach you the most effective way to take down an opponent.

Josephine: Okay, this sounds great, but why do I need to meditate?

Ogard: The physical aspect is only a small part; your powers go way beyond that. Your ability to carry out missions and survive almost completely depends on you controlling their thoughts. To be able to get into your opponent's mind, therefore gaining control of their thoughts. Paralyzing them only lasts a moment; you need to get deep inside their conscious and unconscious mind to gain control of their thoughts. Only then can you truly succeed in your missions. So in order to do that, you must begin with your own.

There is no greater sense of power, no greater strength or achievement than being able to control your own mind. To clear the chaos and silence the noise to focus. It will bring you inner peace and allow you to concentrate on your target.

Josephine: That sounds amazing. I will trust you to guide me and be open to your teachings. You had my parents' trust, now you have mine.

After a few weeks of training, Ogard stopped and looked at Josephine and said, "Tomorrow bring Amalia. She will help you carry out your missions. She doesn't have physical powers, but her intellect is crucial to the tactical parts of your missions. She will need to learn how to defend herself. Your abilities are coming together. You will be ready soon."

Josephine: How will I know what my missions are? And what exactly is my destiny? I'm sorry, but this is all so confusing to me.

"In time you will know. First you must be ready."

Josephine headed back to the sanctuary to tell Amalia that she would be training with her.

When Amalia saw Josephine arrive, she ran over to her and said, "Quick, you need to see this." They went to the back office where the news was on, the story was that of an unknown woman who beat up a man, stole his dog, leaving him in some kind of mental psychotic breakdown. Josephine looked at Amalia and said, "Well, let's just hope it's not me they're talking about." Amalia turned to Josephine, "Of course it's you. Let's hope no one caught you on camera. What should we do? We still have the dog.

Josephine: The dog is staying here, no question. Besides, if they have a camera, they'll see he was beating the dog. I mean . I technically didn't touch the guy.

Amalia tilted her head and stared at Josephine.

Josephine: What? (giggle) Well, I didn't, besides the dude deserved it.

"I'll talk to Ogard when we go train, he'll know how to handle this."

Amalia laughed, "He did deserve it."

Next morning at Ogard's.

Josephine: Did you see the news last night?

Ogard: Yes, we need to find out if there were any witnesses or recordings. Amalia, hack into the city's system and find out if there are any traffic cameras there. If so, review the footage. Check to see if they have drones. I'll make some calls; if need be we will get ahead of it. For now let's train.

Josephine looked at Amalia with her crooked smile and said, "You look nervous."

"I am, look at these noodle arms, please be gentle."

Training went well, Amalia kicked butt. After a few weeks, we both came a long way with our fighting skills.

Josephine has been able to master the art of meditation, allowing her to gain control of her powers. her strength has increased, along with her agility. We are now ready to introduce weapons training.

Ogard takes us into the weapons room, "Pick out some small weapons you can easily conceal and your main weapon of choice." I should speak to you. As I looked around, I noticed a crossbow. I could envision myself in a battle using it. It wasn't too big, and I was able to shoot with perfect precision. The arrows were tipped with tranquilizers, so that I could put the perpetrators to sleep, not kill them.

Amalia, went straight for a hand gun that shot tranqs and a retractable nightstick that doubled as a taser. We chose a few more smaller weapons and continued on training.

As the day passed, I was becoming one with my powers. Increasing my strength, all my senses were heightened.

Amalia and I were at the sanctuary, wrapping things up for the evening when we hear the news talking about dairy farms in Florida torturing cows. They were playing small clips of video they took while engaging in the abuse. I instantly felt enraged, hurt, and confused. Amalia felt the same. We spoke of what we would do, how we can make this right.

A few days later, we hear of a couple who were abusing thirteen children, depriving them of food and beating, raping, and mentally destroying them. All while teaching children in our public-school system and going completely unnoticed.

Storms were brewing all over, fires in California, a North Korean tyrant starving and killing his own people, afflicting fear to the world with threats of nuclear weapons, antagonizing war.

I felt distraught, helpless, angry, and sad. We have to do something; things have to change.

The next morning at training, Ogard could tell something was bothering me. I expressed my concerns, how I wish I could do more. I set up my animal sanctuary to do some good, to save animals and provide a place where elderly, children, and people with disabilities could come and play with animals, feed them, and feel like they have a purpose. A safe, happy place to make a difference, but it's not enough. With all these horrible things happening in the world. Storms, earthquakes, fires, flood, mass shootings, terrorism, threats of war. The unraveling of our law and order. All happening at once. I feel as though evil is winning. The scales are tilted. Somehow we need to restore balance.

Ogard: Come with me, I need to show you something. Amalia, you come, too.

We walked past his back yard into the forest. Hidden among the trees, there was a rock formation. Agard moved a boulder to reveal an entry way into a cave of some sort. There were stairs that lead down. I could hear running water. Sounded like a waterfall. At the bottom, there was a small natural pool. To the right of it was a workshop.

Ogard: This is where I come to work.

He went to a cabinet and made some tea. Drink this, close your eyes, and clear your mind of all thoughts. Come kneel by the pool and place your hand in the water.

Josephine: Okay? This is weird, just saying.

We laughed.

Ogard: Keep your mind open, Josephine.

She took the tea and drank it, kneeled by the pool, took a nice long, deep breath, closed her eyes, and placed her hand in the water. She began to have a vision. She could see her mother with a man in a robe. He was saying he knew of her struggles. She and her husband were trying to conceive but couldn't. He said he could help her bear a child. He would bless her with a pregnancy, but the child would be his and Demeter. The child would not be ordinary. She is destined to save humanity from itself. To serve justice and bring hope back to mankind. To protect and serve the innocents.

My mother, so desperate to bear a child, agreed. She became pregnant.

She said, "I can see so much hurt in the world, a darkness coming over it. You are seeing and feeling what our baby can see."

"Your husband must not know. Before you give birth, we must meet. There's a great deal of important information and responsibility. But for now, enjoy your pregnancy. Your daughter will have powers. Though she's a child of the Gods, her human side will make her vulnerable. It is imperative that no one knows. For it could put her in danger.

The woman began to speak, "When she is of age, she will be trained on how to use and control her powers. We will learn of her destiny and will receive all that she needs to fulfill it. Until then you must conceal her abilities, suppress her powers. This will keep her powers suppressed. You must give her some every day." My mother took the bottle and agreed.

"I have so many questions."

"In time we will answer your questions. You can give her the human name of your choosing. Her Goddess name is Lenox."

Amalia could see my vision in the pool. I came out of my vision and asked for more tea. I need to know more.

Ogard: In time, Lenox, just know you are here to tilt the scales of justice. Evil will not win. Amalia, you have been chosen to help Lenox in carrying out her missions. With your high intellect, loyalty, and hacking abilities, you will play an integral part in the success of the missions.

Over the next couple of weeks, they trained hard. Krav Maga came easy to Lenox; she was becoming one with her true self. The crossbow was her favorite weapon. She could take down any target with precision. Amalia reconfigured the arrow tips to tranquilizers. The opponents would be put to sleep. It was genius. We want to punish evil. Death would only end their misery. They need to feel all the pain, the suffering, the fear they caused.

Jail isn't punishment, free meals, room and board, a gym, a library, free medical, clothes on their backs. The criminals have it better than half the hard-working citizens of this world. Only when they feel what they have done, every bit of physical pain, mental anguish, the fears and sorrow of their victims. Every bit of it. They will relive the torture over and over again until they repent. Truly repent, or they will stay for eternity in a padded room living in anguish.

That is real justice, as they are living it; it will take the pain and memory from the victims, so that they can regain their innocence.

That is true justice.

We began to lay out our first mission. We started investigating the farms. Amalia pulled up aerial maps of the farms to see the layouts while Josephine called reporters to get details on the horrific events.

While Amalia was able to tap into the camera system and disable the lights, Josephine took a ride out to the farms. She went in to speak to the people in charge. They were cold to her, denying the allegations and claiming that the person in question was no longer employed there.

As Josephine walked back to her jeep, she was approached by one of the farm hands. He pretended to shake her hand to give her a thumbdrive.

"Here is the information you're looking for, proof of the abuse. The people on the videos still work here. Please, if there is a way you can help. I need this job, but I can't keep witnessing these horrific acts. I'll try to assist further if possible."

The owner was walking up.

"Oh, you have a boyfriend. Lucky guy." The farm hand said loudly to ensure he was heard.

Josephine smiled, whispered, "Thank you. I will do what I can."

Farm hand ; "She's a pretty girl, I had to try."

"Get back to work. The owner yelled."

On her drive back to the sanctuary, Josephine looked at the thumbdrive. She wanted to know what was on it but was fearful of its contents. Whatever it is, we will end it.

When she got back, her and Amalia conferenced Ogard. They watched the contents. The images were worse than anything she could have imagined. Tears came down their faces. She shut it off. "I've seen enough. Tomorrow night we shall deliver punishment. Justice will be served. Prepare the back fields to accommodate the cattle and round up the rescue teams and trucks."

We headed to Ogard's to get our weapons. He took us to the hidden room where the weapons were kept. When we got there, he took us through a secret passageway to a room that contained uniforms, or shall I say disguises.

Ogard: It is imperative that you are not recognized. This mask will not only disguise your face, but it will heighten your senses. The outfit is like armor. It will keep you protected. Choose your accessories, each one has a different function. Choose small hand-held weapons that you can carry and access easily. Amalia, this one for you. It will keep you protected and conceal your identity. Go put them on, and I will explain how they work.

The ladies went behind the screen to put on their gear. When Lenox put on her disguise and looked at the mirror, a light with a bright glow started from her feet to her head and blinded her. When she reopened her eyes, the outfit had turned pure white with gold accents. It was a corset with an open back, a large cross tattoo appeared across her entire back with the words, "In God I trust" through the middle. The shorts were also white, the boots were thigh high white boots with gold sole and heels. She had a garter that held a knife and taser pens. The heels of the boots were jetted for quick escape. She had two arm bands, one for each side; one had slots to hold things, the other was given removable rings each with different functions. Lastly she put on her mask; it covered the left side of her face and from the nose up and her eye on her left. A glow moved up to her face and fizzled out. Lenox was bigger, taller, stronger. She could feel her energy surging through her body. She closed her eyes and had a vision of herself talking to the gods, Zeus and Demeter

Zeus: Please take special care, my child, you possess my strength and my powers, as well as Demeter's empath abilities and her earth mother powers. Her compassion for humanity. You are the only chance the human race has to survive.

She opened her eyes, and they were gone.

Amalia put on her jumpsuit; the same cross appeared on the base of her neck. Her lapel has a button on it that has different functions. She wore knee socks and knee-high combat boots. Her boots had pockets and compartments to hold weapons and tools. Amalia also wore a mask. Hers covers just her eyes up to her forehead, leaving her nose and bottom half of her face exposed. It was fierce.

We went to show Ogard. He started to explain what each component did.

"Lenox, you have two arms bands; this one with pockets contains a master key that can open anything, a mini telescope, and a compass.

The other one–"

Lenox interrupts, "Why do I recognize these rings?"

Ogard laughs, "Look closer." She took a closer look and realized they were the Patriots Super Bowl rings. "Well, I figured since you're a little Masshole Pats fan, I'd throw something a little special in."

Lenox and Amalia laughed, "That's awesome." But my boy is here in Florida now so I need one more to represent him.

"Each ring is removable, and they are not really rings obviously. This one is a smoke bomb, zip line, sleeping gas, laser, and grenades.

The crosses that appear on you will help shield you from harm, make it difficult for anyone to hurt you physically. But it's not impossible, so you have to stay vigilant at all times. Amalia, now it's imperative that you remember you do not have super powers. Though I must say your brain is a super power. It will not keep you from getting physically harmed, so you must be careful. Stay under the radar. Your lapel has two buttons, one creates a force field that will create an impenetrable bubble around you. The other is a laser. On your belt, there is a hidden tranq gun. In your boots, you have master keys, data sticks, whatever else you may need to tap into their systems to manipulate them to suit our needs."

When she arrived at the sanctuary, Ogard and Amalia were waiting up front.

Amalia: Are you okay?

Josephine: Not really, as she shakes her head. But I will be. Gather the crew, have them get the fields ready, we will give these animals the respect they deserve. Make sure there's plenty of food and the vets on staff.

She turned to Ogard and Amalia, "A $300 fine, that's what they call justice. What a joke. All life should be respected. If you can't do that, I will seek you out. You will know what true punishment is."

Over the next few days, Detective Coutone managed to arrange a meeting. Meanwhile Amalia and Josephine trained day and night.

It was the night before. Josephine decided to walk through the forest to clear her head.

Josephine looked up to the sky and said, "God, I wish I could speak to my parents. Mom always knew how to reassure me. She taught me to always trust my instincts. My dad gave me confidence. He made me believe I could accomplish anything I set my mind to. I miss you guys so much." She closed her eyes and felt a warm tear run down her face, followed by a soft gentle finger wiping it away. It was Demeter, my goddess mother.

Demeter: I feel your pain, my child. The pain you feel, I also feel. We will continue to feel this pain as long as the world is in chaos. You are stronger and more powerful than you could ever imagine. Your ability to feel the pain and sorrows of the world may feel like a curse at times, but it is what makes you so great and destined to restore the balance of good and evil. Use that pain to unlock your great powers. Your powers, your strength, your extraordinary compassion for all life, the combination of my powers, Zeus, and your human surrogates make you the most powerful of all.

Continue to follow Ogard's lead, follow your heart, and listen to your instincts. They will not fail you. With each mission, you will restore some balance to the earth and humanity. Earth is near extinction, and you were created with love to save it. To stop humans from destroying themselves and everything in their realm. The time is here for you to carve your path, you're Lenox Savior of Humanity. Now go get some sleep, you have your first mission tomorrow.

The next morning, we headed to the farms. As the employees began to gather into the community center, Josephine looked at their faces and body language. Some looked annoyed, others looked happy to be taking a break from their work, some with a look of concern.

Once the room was filled, Amalia went to find the transformer that powered the farms. Josephine and Ogard entered the room. Ogard stayed back by the doors.

Officer Coutone was at the front with the farm owners. They laid out the reason for the meeting and began to introduce Josephine. Some started to laugh and make comments, like this is a waste of time, bullshit, they're animals, who cares? Josephine became infuriated and gave Amalia the go ahead to cut the power.

Everything went dark, Ogard secured the doors, so no one could escape. Josephine transformed into Lenox. She closed her eyes and raised her arms up, the ground was trembling. Lights began to burst, and people started to scramble in fear.

One of the ring leaders grabbed a 2x4 and went after Lenox. She kicked the board right out of his hands and dove through his legs, knocking him to the floor, then punching him in the throat. Another came up behind her; she jumped right to her feet, turned, and put his arm behind his back, smashing his head against another man's nose. Blood started to gush down his face as he put his hand over his face. People were screaming and scattering trying to get out. Lenox spun and flung the man into the wall. She took out her cross bow and shot the back-up generator, so they couldn't get the power back up.

She closed her eyes, energy soared through her body. The room walls shaking and ground trembling, power lines began to burst outside. The men fell to their knees, some on their sides in agonizing pain for they were living through the horror they inflicted on those innocent creatures. They could feel their anuses ripping, their intestines being punctured by rusty pipes. They could feel unbearable fear and confusion while being buried to head height in ditches left to drown in the rain storms, unable to move while the water rises.

Totally aware of the fear and pain, bound by chains unable to run, unable to move, their bodies cramping. Tears would run as they watched their young calves being brutally beaten to death in front of them, followed by prolonged periods of starvation and dehydration. It was endless torture, both mental and physical. These monsters were agonizing in pain, feeling the reality of what they had done. The beatings and torture, over and over again. they couldn't escape the excruciating pain, unable to mentally detach themselves.

Some of them rose up from the ground in confusion. Their pain had stopped but they were left with a feeling of shame for they had witnessed the horror and failed to act to protect the innocent animals from being brutalized. Therefore it was as if they committed the acts themselves by allowing it to happen. They vowed to themselves and to God that they would never stand idly by while such injustice is happening in front of them. The pain, the guilt, the torture felt all too real. They vowed to never do it again and begged for forgiveness. In doing so, they were released. But those who were pure evil remained in the state of torture. They continued convulsing on the ground, wrenching in pain.

Lenox took a deep breath when she heard the sirens. She needed to escape. Amalia grabbed her things, released the locks, and ran toward the van.

She looked back at Lenox, "Keep going," she told her, "get out of here." Lenox took off, running at lightning speed through the fields. Her boots propelled her. She made it back to the sanctuary as Josephine, just in time to greet Officer Coutone.

Josephine: Hi, officer, what can I do for you?

Officer Coutone: I wanted to make sure you were okay; things got chaotic back at the farm, and I didn't see you leave.

Josephine: I managed to get out when the lights went out before all the doors were locked. I wasn't sure what was going on, so I got out of there. Was going to call you later.

Officer Coutone: Well, I'm glad you're okay. And I wanted to let you know that the perps got what was coming to them.

Josephine: How so? We didn't even get to have the meeting.

Officer Coutone: Well, mother nature unleashed fury over there. Ground tremors caused powerlines to burst and fires started. When things calmed down, the perps were on the ground shaking in some kind of catatonic state. They were taken to the hospital. If they don't snap out of it, they'll probably be committed to the mental ward. Anyway, just thought you'd want to know. Also, I need to ask for your help.

Josephine: Yes, of course, what is it?

Officer Coutone: We were wondering since the farms will be out of commission for a while if you could house the animals here at your sanctuary? At least until we find another solution.

Josephine: Yes, it would be my pleasure. I'll send my crews out right now.

Ogard and Amalia came outside when they saw the officer speaking to Josephine.

Josephine looked at them and smiled.

"Officer Coutone just asked if we could house the farm animals."

The officer didn't know that the arrangements were already made.

"We will get the crew ready and head out there."

Officer Coutone: Thank you, thank you for everything.

Josephine smiled as the officer excused himself and left.

They went inside and all let out a sigh of relief.

Ogard: This is good. It's less likely that they will ever think you were involved in what happened.

As the crews came back with the animals and got them settled, Josephine took a deep breath. She felt a sense of relief and pain, for she could feel the animals' fears and pain.

She pressed her forehead on a cow's forehead and whispered, "You're going to be okay".

She turned to Ogard and said, "I wish I could erase their pain."

Ogard: You can, Josephine, you are just tapping the surface of your powers. The more we train, as you learn who you are, you will be able to better control your powers and unlock more of them. You will be able to use them in the most unimaginable ways.

This brought me a sense of peace. They went inside and put on some music. Amalia and Josephine began to dance all goofy. Ogard laughed and shook his head.

"Amalia soooo cannot dance, ha-ha."

Leskha walks in, turns the music down, and turns on the TV.

"Breaking news. A couple who were tried for abusing thirteen kids got off on a technicality. They cannot be retried."

Josephine: Looks like we have our next mission.

Disappointed, she turned to Ogard and Amalia.

"We have work to do." Leskha, being a mother, was especially bothered.

On the verge of tears, "I can't stand by and do nothing. I want in. I'll do whatever I have to help bring these monsters to justice. All acts of evil have consequences, and I won't stop until I serve justice for all that is innocent and defenseless.

# A WORLD IN CHAOS

In the morning, Josephine awoke and immediately began to research the Kurkin's case. She needed to know exactly what they did. What she discovered was horrific in every way. The abuse began twenty-nine years ago when Louise delivered her first child. They took pleasure in inflicting pain and terror on their child. It sexually aroused them, so they continued to have children to add to their sadistic pleasure and foreplay.

Josephine needs to go to California and see the children. She wants to read their journals to truly understand the extent of damage and pain they endured. Not only to deliver justice but to find a way to erase those memories so the children have a chance of living a normal life going forward.

Josephine got ready and headed to the Sanctuary; on her way, she called leskha and Ogard to have them meet. She wants to strategize to come up with a plan on how to infiltrate the judicial system to find out where they went wrong. How could such creatures who are capable of such heinous acts get off?

At the Sanctuary, the four of them began to discuss the details of the case. Leskha was having difficulties listening to what the children endured. This compassion and empathy will give her the strength needed to carry out the mission.

Ogard scheduled for them to get to train later. Josephine still had a lot to learn about the power of Lenox. Amalia and Leskha need training on their fighting and weapons skills.

Later, when they arrived at Ogards, Leskha and Amalia started to train on their fighting skills. Josephine decided to go for a walk through the forest to clear her head. She still had so many unanswered questions about who she is and her powers. She needed to better understand her purpose, so that the most good could come out of her missions. As she walked to the forest, her mind went into a meditative state. She soon felt like she was floating, and when she slowly blinked her eyes, there was Demeter.

Demeter took her hand, "Your heart is heavy, my child. Your purpose will become more clear with each mission. Trust in yourself and let your feelings rule your power. Your heart is heavy because there is so much turmoil in the world, and you want to fix it. One day at a time, one mission at a time, that's how you will fix it. With every innocent you help, you are sending the power of positivity through the world, and the universe will respond. Don't worry about the big picture right now. It'll all come together. You possess my empath ability, Zeus's strengths and powers, your earth mother's intuition, and your own fire. Use your pain, your love, and your intellect. Once you harness all your strengths, you will be most powerful. And nothing, no one, will be able to stop you from saving humanity."

I opened my eyes, and she was gone, as I headed back to the house it began to rain.

Josephine jumped right in with the ladies and picked up a baton and went after Ogard jokingly. He began to spar with her, complementing how far she had come when she managed to knock his weapon from his hands and pin him up against a tree.

Josephine to Ogard, "I want to learn how to control my ability to make the ground shake."

Ogard, "You not only can make the ground where you are shake, but when you tap into the inner workings of your mind, you can make the earth shake and split the ground like an earthquake and shifting plates.

"Let's go into the forest and practice, ladies, take a break and come with." They all walked into the forest and stopped when they arrived at a clearing, there were little trees and big boulders.

Ogard, "We're going to start by having you shake and split the boulders. You have to really focus on the boulder. Let everything else fade into the background. Forget the trees, the ground, us, everything. Let that all be a blur."

Josephine took a deep breath and began to focus. She zoned in on the boulder and tried to let the rest of the forest fade out. She was thinking about the pain and fear those children must be facing, and so, the ground began to tremble.

Ogard, "Easy try to control it and isolate the boulder."

Josephine focused in on the boulder, and it began to shake; she wanted to split it in half. It was shaking harder when it suddenly burst into a million pieces. They had to run for cover. Some of the stone fragments were severing tree limbs flying everywhere. When it settled, they got up and looked at each other.

Ogard, "We're going to need to practice this a little more." They all started to laugh.

Amalia, "So cool though, super bad ass."

The next morning, Amalia began to research the case and get un-disclosed information about the extent of the abuse and torture. We needed to get as much detail as possible, so when we apprehend the couple, Lenox could deliver the appropriate justice. We also need to locate them since they disappeared once the case was rendered a mistrial. The district attorneys were scrambling to build a new case with other charges in hopes of getting some justice but so far have been unsuccessful.

When Josephine arrived, Amalia briefed Josephine on the specifics. David and Louise Kurkin started abusing their first child twenty-nine years ago. They took pleasure in hurting their child and would become sexually aroused when they would inflict pain. So they continued to have children to abuse and torture. The children were shackled to the beds, their pets were starved to death and beaten in front of them to instill more fear and gain complete control.

They were sexually abusing them in addition to the beatings, star-vation, being burnt with cigarettes, locked in the basement with no provisions or light for days sometimes more than a week, left to soil themselves repeatedly. The extent of the abuse was heinous, so sa-distic, that it is difficult to comprehend how such evil could exist. They had multiple fractures that had healed and fractured again.

Josephine just thought to herself, how did they manage to survive? Amalia could see the level of distress on her face.

Amalia, "Are you okay?"

Josephine looked at Amalia and replied, "I am, and they will be, too. Call the detectives and district attorneys on the case and tell them I am an investigative reporter and want to assist in finding them and getting evidence from leads provided by my sources. Create a fake identity for me with all the necessary credentials needed to pass a background check. I'm going to head over to Ogard's later to see if I can somehow erase the bad memories from the kids to help them heal. They need a chance at a normal life."

Josephine was wrapping things up when a staff member approached and mentioned that the group leader for the children's group that participated in today's feed and play program for rescue dogs and cats wanted a moment of her time.

Josephine, "Yeah, sure, is everything okay?"

Staff, "I believe so, the kids are enjoying themselves. But trust me, you want to talk to him. Serious eye candy."

They laughed.

Josephine, "You're so bad."

Josephine walked to the dog and cat rescue center when she locked eyes with one of the most gorgeous men she had ever seen. Wow, she thought to herself. She wasn't kidding. He's HOT.

Josephine, "Hi, I'm Josephine, how can, how can I help you?" She uttered nervously.

"Hi, I'm Lincoln. Thank you for taking the time to talk to me. I run this youth program. It's early intervention to keep kids on the right path. I just wanted to shake your hand and tell you I think what you do here is wonderful. Would you happen to have time for a quick lunch while the kids are occupied?"

Josephine, "Um, sure, I have about 45 minutes or so."

They started walking to the lunch area, and Josephine had to admit she felt nervous butterflies in her stomach. Her hands were even a little sweaty. Dang, he's sweet, too.

They sat down and began chatting with her best poker face of course. He was kind of rambling, hmm, could he be nervous, too? She wondered. They ordered a snack, and he continued to chat about how wonderful her Sanctuary and programs are.

Lincoln, "I'm just saying, we need more kindness and understanding in the world. I was in Miami for a conference, and this guy started spewing hate speech about the gay, transsexual community. It was horrible. He was expressing how he wanted to do something to teach them a lesson and send a message."

Something in Josephine sparked, and she began to ask questions in concern.

"Did you get the guy's name? Any details on what he was planning?"

Lincoln, "No, I kind of dismissed him as a drunk bigot. The bartender said he goes there often and is rumored to be hooking up with trans girls, so I figured he was just self-loathing. I just wanted to get away from him so things didn't escalate since what he was saying was making me angry."

Josephine's gut was telling her to look into the incident further. Something's not right, and this man is making what I consider to be a terroristic threat against this community.

"What restaurant was this?"

Lincoln, "Oasis it's on Ocean Boulevard. Why?"

Josephine, "No reason, just curious. So how long have you been working with children?"

They continued with pleasant conversation as they walked back to the kids.

Lincoln, "It was great to meet you. I never do this, but would you have dinner with me sometime?" He looked so nervous and vulnerable as he put himself out there.

Josephine hesitated when she noticed the death glare from her staff. "Yeah, sure. My schedule is a bit crazy right now."

Lincoln, "No pressure, whenever is good for you."

"Okay. Well I'll be leaving for California for a little while, maybe before I leave. I'll confirm and let you know."

Lincoln, "Sounds great," he gave her his card, and she headed back to the office to talk to Amalia.

Josephine, "So I just had a quick lunch with this guy Lincoln that's here with his kids group, and he mentioned something that is bugging me." She explained about the man and his hate spew. "It could be nothing but definitely worth looking into a little. If this guy really is planning an attack, we need to figure out what and stop him."

Amalia, "Got it. I'll look into it as soon as I confirm your California trip. Your identity is all good to go. I put in the call to the police department and the DA's office. They are on board and will graciously accept any help they can get."

Josephine, "That's good work. Thank you."

Josephine headed to Ogard's to fill him in on the progress, and she really wanted to work on her ability to erase the painful memories from the innocent victims. When she got there, he was in the kitchen making tea. It was an herbal tea that would help me relax, so I could meditate and harness my energy.

As I filled him in on the progress while sipping our tea, I got a call from Amalia.

Amalia, "So I called the bar where your friend Lincoln was at and talked to two bartenders. They said that the guy's name is Omar Fant. For weeks said he's been talking about shooting up the gay community, Rambling on and on. He has been in Miami for work but lives in Orlando. He figured he was just talking nonsense when drunk, trying to throw off suspicion of him being gay because he's married. He's seen him leave with trans girls and was rumored to hit the clubs and hook up with trans women a lot. It wasn't until a few nights ago when he rambled on about scoring a lot of semi-automatic weapons."

"Alright , I'm going to head to Miami and do some digging. If this guy is serious, we have to stop him. Find out where he is staying and get his home address and where he hangs out at home."

Ogard, "What's going on?"

Josephine, "This man was at the Sanctuary with his kids group and told me about a guy who was rambling about a possible attack on the gay-transgender community. Want to see if it's a credible threat. Put a stop to it, if it is."

Ogard, "Okay, let me know if you need me to come with once you get more information."

They finished their tea and headed to the cave to work on her mind control ability. When they got there, she went down to the spring and put her hands in the water. Her mind began to drift as she imagined herself clearing the pain and fear from the children.

When she opened her eyes, she looked over at Ogard.

Josephine, "I would like to practice to see if I can do it. Is there anything in your past that troubles you?"

Ogard, "There are many things I have felt and seen that have troubled me. But I wouldn't change a thing. With the bad, I had a lot of good. Not like those children who have only experienced the bad. They never had a chance to know what good is."

Josephine, "I get that, but there has to be one thing. Something so painful that you can't bear to think about. We all have something we would like to erase. Mine is the death of my human parents."

Ogard, "Well my biggest regret was not being able to save my wife and unborn child."

Josephine, "I didn't know you were married before and lost them, I'm so sorry."

Ogard, "I don't speak of it much, see, I was away on a lot of missions, I didn't realize that where we lived in Minnesota was toxic grounds with nuclear waste products. It was in the water source and in our soils, our food. For me it mutated my genes, so I am no longer immortal. Now when I use my powers, I age rapidly, which I learned to live with and so I contribute by mentoring young heroes like yourself to find their way. For my wife and unborn child, it was different. She got very sick, got cancer that rapidly spread through other parts of her body. They were unable to save her but managed to save the baby. Unfortunately he only lived for two days. She was only about seven months along, and all his organs weren't completely developed, so they had him on machines, a feeding tube, but they quickly realized that he also had cancer and was not strong enough to fight it...I've always felt responsible, I had chosen to live there. Thinking it was a safe place to have a family."

Josephine, "You couldn't control that then; information on the grounds wasn't as accessible like today with the internet. You can't blame yourself."

Ogard, "I was a superhero, Able to fight villains and protect the citizens, but I failed to recognize the dangers I put my family in. I failed them."

Josephine, "You shouldn't feel that way. There was no way you could have known. And I'm sure they are proud of you watching from the heavens for all your sacrifices. Is this why you are alone? Afraid to love again?"

Ogard, "It is certainly a big part of it."

Josephine, "Let me practice on you, I'll only focus on that aspect of your life. Because I agree with you, the pains we go through, our survival, gives us strength and drive. It makes us stronger and smarter. But some pain is too debilitating, if we can't make peace with it, let it go. It will start to consume you in some way. Like it is you."

Ogard, "Okay, you can try; after all I'm here to help you grow."

Josephine took his hands and looked deep into his eyes. She could feel herself turning into Lenox, the tattoo appeared on her back, and she was suddenly towering over Ogard. She looked deeper into his eyes and could feel his heart ache, the guilt he had been carrying all these years. The gaping hole in his soul and heart that was once occupied by the joy of his family.

Suddenly they were floating in what felt like another realm. His mind was open, and Lenox was able to steer his thoughts into a more positive space, so that he could see this tragedy as an opportunity to do more good in the world. She was able to channel his pain not to make him forget, but to see it in a different light. Then he could love again and have a more balanced life. Completeness.

She closed her eyes, and when she reopened them, she was Josephine and they were back in the cave near the spring. Ogard could hear the trickle of the water and a feeling of tranquility consumed him.

Josephine, "Are you okay? How are you feeling?"

Ogard, "My heart feels lighter, and my senses are heightened. I don't know ? I need a moment to process"

Ogard went up the stairs and outside. As he stepped outside the cave, he felt the breeze on his face and through his hair. He could smell the freshness of the forest in the air and hear the leaves rustling. In the distance were the sounds of birds singing. He took a deep breath and just absorbed the beauty of the earth. His mind was clear and heart was light. He could once again enjoy the small preciousness of nature that was smothered by his pain. Though he still had a vivid memory of his loving wife, child, and the tragedy that took them, he no longer held the burden of feeling responsible for their deaths. He was set free from his anguish. Able to accept it and understand that it was all part of a bigger plan.

Josephine wanted to go after him, but she decided to stay back to give him his space.

When he returned back to the cave, he thanked her. It was the best he has felt in a very long time.

Ogard, "I'm looking forward to heading to California to serve justice for those children. Let's figure out Miami and head there Monday."

Josephine, "Amalia is looking into travel plans. Have Leskha come everyday to prepare her both mentally and physically."

Josephine left and headed back to the sanctuary. On the way her phone rang, she didn't recognize the number but decided to answer. It was Lincoln.

Lincoln, "Hi again, I hope you don't mind me calling. I enjoyed our brief lunch chat and was wondering if you would consider going to dinner with me sometime before you leave for California.

Josephine smiled, feeling giddy inside.

Josephine, "I'd like that. I'll let you know when I return from California." Unfortunately something came up and it will have to wait till I return.

Over the next couple days, Leskha trained with Ogard while Amalia arranged travel plans to California and Miami.

On Thursday Josephine and Amalia arrive at the Miami Airport. Josephine rented a convertible Camaro, and they headed for Miami Beach. We headed straight to Oasis where Joe, the bartender we spoke to works. They walk up to the hostess.

Josephine, "Hi, is Joe working?"

Hostess, "Yeah, he's the one with the mohawk at the bar."

Josephine, "Thanks."

They walk up to the bar and introduce themselves.

Josephine, "HI, I'm Josephine, and this is my assistant Amalia. We spoke to you a couple days ago about that patron that was talking hate speech."

Joe, Oh, yeah, how can I help you?"

Josephine, "We work with anti hate crimes and want to ask you a few more questions about the guy that was here spewing hate speech and possible threats against the gay community."

Joe, "Okay ya I remember that guy, what would you like to know?"

Josephine, "How often does he come here ? Has he always talked like that? His full name? Basically anything you know would be helpful."

Joe, "Let me get someone to cover, and we'll go sit at a table and chat."

They sat at the table.

Joe came over and sat down.

Joe, "You know at first I thought he was just a miserable drunk full of hate. He started coming around mostly on Thursdays and Fridays for work. I know he lives in Orlando. Can't say first hand, but the rumor is that he frequents tranny bars and is in the closet, hooks up with them on the down low. So I don't know if it is just his way of covering his tracks, throwing people off about his sexuality, or if he's really nuts and will do something terrible. I'm not sure what his full name is."

Amalia, "Did he pay with a credit card?"

Joe, "Yeah, but I don't know how to look that up."

Amalia, "Is your system online? If it is, I can look up the receipts to see if any match his name. From there I can get his information and pull up his photo, so we know what he looks like."

Joe, "Oh, okay, great, what do you need from me?"

Amalia; "The IP address," Joe looked at her funny, Obviously not knowing how to retrieve the Ip address. Amalia; "I'll walk you through it."

They laughed. While they got the information, he happened to walk in.

Josephine to Joe, "Act natural. Don't worry."

Josephine sat next to him at the bar while Amalia worked on looking up his information.

Joe served him and started small talk, "What's up, Omar ,what's good for the weekend? Are you staying around here?"

Omar, "Nah, man, I'm heading back to Orlando, I have some business to take care of."

Josephine, "Sorry to interrupt, I'll be in Orlando this weekend. Do you recommend any clubs or places to go?"

Omar looked at her and said, "Well it depends on what you like. There are a lot of places."

Josephine, "Do you know of any good gay night clubs? My friends prefer it."

Omar's demeanor completely changed. He turned to Josephine and said, "You can always go to Pulse. I hear that's good."

Josephine, "Great, thanks, will I see you there?"

Omar, "You just might."

Josephine smiled and thanked Joe.

Joe, "Let me know if you need anything. Here's my number, call me if you get in any trouble. Be careful."

Josephine, "Always." She gave home a smile and looked at Amalia.

Amalia, "I got what I need.

They left and headed up to Orlando. "Let's get there before him, so we can scope out his house. See what we can find."

We get to his apartment and pick the locks. We look through his closets, dresser drawers trying to find anything that will let us into his state of mind. He had a laptop on his desk, so Amalia started on figuring out his passwords to see if we could find something. We didn't find any evidence of weapon purchases, or bomb materials so this was our last hope to get some insight on what he is planning.

Amalia got in and started digging. It took her a minute, but she was able to recover erased searches on gun stocks, homosexual erotic pornography, and religious hate speech. We also found notes on his personal calendar, all referenced homosexual activities in and around Miami and Orlando area. He was definitely obsessed. Most of the things we found were explicitly violent. They both had a horrible feeling in their guts. That combined with the way he looked at Josephine when she pretended to be gay was enough to confirm their suspicion. Everything was telling her to look further. when they found searches on Pulse and its activities.

They decided to look into Pulse nightclub; they researched the layout, security, and called to see what the theme was for the night. It was a masquerade party. Couldn't be more perfect.

"I'll go as Lenox and you go as Amalia. We will fit right in. But...that means he will be in costume also, and I didn't see anything here, so we will have to be extra vigilant to locate him."

We headed over to the nightclub after closing to see what kind of security systems they have and alter the locks on the doors so that they only lock from the outside and not inside. Amalia accessed the cameras so she could watch it from her phone.

They arrived at the club at 11:30 pm; there was a long line. Everyone was dressed in outlandish fun and fabulous outfits. Lenox, being a seven foot 4 inch tall amazon goddess, was getting serious attention. Combined with being next to Amalia, a whole 4'11", everyone was commenting on how cute she was. People were so joyous and friendly. Just out for a night of light fun. Lenox couldn't understand why anyone would want to inflict harm on them. But she wasn't going to let it happen.

The night went on, and they were making friends, dancing, blending into the crowd careful to not draw attention. Lenox can dance.

"Oh, yeah, play me some Daddy Yankee, and I'll break it down," she said to Amalia.

Amalia was cracking up.

Amalia, "I don't have that gene. Can't dance."

Her smart watch started to buzz. It had recognized Omar; he didn't come in a mask, so our facial recognition spotted him on the balcony. He was wearing a trench coat. Lenox made her way to him, and they locked eyes.

He ripped his trench coat open and pulled out a rifle; it looked like he altered it into a fully automatic weapon. Lenox jumped in the air over the crowd. Everyone was in awe and thought it was part of a show. A sea of bullets were flying. Lenox used a force field and pushed them up to the ceiling. The bullets were deflected and held up. Lenox signaled down to Amalia to clear the club. Amalia set off the alarms and sprinkler system, getting everyone to go outside. Omar dropped the rifle and pulled out a glock trying to shoot Lenox, but she was too quick. She sprung towards him, the bullets dropping from the ceiling, and she grabbed him by the neck. She squeezed his neck and lifted him up, his eyes bulging. For a brief second, she wanted to squeeze the life out him. He dropped his gun, and she looked at his eyes and got into his mind. He began to feel pain, fear that he inflicted on other victims. An overwhelming guilt came over him. For him this feeling was unbearable. It meant he was weak and failing the cause.

Lenox, "Why did you do this?" She wanted to get into his mind but then she heard the sirens, and she knew she had to get out there before they see her. She tied him up and dropped him. He laid there convulsing, vomiting from the guilt. Thoughts of suicide crossed his mind.

"I'm weak, I failed my god," he wailed. Lenox left his weapons so police could try to uncover who he was working for or with.

She ran outside, grabbed Amalia, and they got out of there.

Lenox: "Amalia I need you to erase all the footage that we are in just leave the part of him with his weapon."

Amalia, "I'm on it. It'll take me a couple minutes."

Lenox, "Something else is going on. This wasn't an isolated hate crime against gays. He's just a pawn. A part of something bigger. I'm happy we saved these people. But we have to figure out who really was behind this. When we get back from California, we need to investigate further.

When they got to the hotel, Lenox was back to Josephine. They walked into the lobby and the news was on. People circled around the TV.

"Are you seeing this? There was some kind of attempted shooting." Everyone thought it was a show. "Crazy shit. They are saying some amazon in white saved them. Police think they were hallucinations from drugs. But they were going to look into it. They had the suspect in custody with the weapons. He was babbling nonsense. They cuffed him to a stretcher and brought him to the hospital with police detail.

Police officer, "Bullets are everywhere! I don't know how everyone got out unharmed. Unbelievable!"

Josephine and Amalia looked at each other and said, "Let's get to the room."

In the elevator on the way up, Amalia re-revised the security footage to make sure neither one of them were there.

Amalia, "I almost died when the cop said they were hallucinating on drugs. If we weren't in it we would probably say the same thing."

Josephine laughing, "I know, the whole thing sounds pretty ridiculous when you think about it. I still have a hard time grasping it. It's so weird, I remember everything, but it's like watching it from the outside."

They get to the room and turn the TV on to see what they are saying about the incident. So far they are dismissing the witnesses talking about the Amazon in white and looking at the evidence for a more conclusive story, which is great news for Lenox since she does not yet want to be known.

The next morning, they flew back to Clearwater and got ready for California.

They decided to meet at the sanctuary and leave from there when Leskha arrived.

She said, "Did you hear what they are saying on the news? They are saying that the suspect is connected to ISIS and that his attempted failed attack wasn't an isolated hate crime but an act of terrorism."

Josephine, "So my feeling was right, it is part of a bigger thing. When we get back, we need to investigate further into ISIS. Find out their agenda.

Leskha, "From what they said on the news, I gather that ISIS is a terrorist group that is attacking all American culture that they deem is immoral. Our way of life in general. Our freedom of religion. Our "materialistic ways", Americana.

Josephine, "Well then when we get back, we will investigate and end them."

They headed to the airport, onto California.

Amalia researched the Kurkin's history to see if we could find clues as to where they could be hiding.

"We could always try interviewing the children, but most of them are so damaged, we're not sure how much help they will be in finding them."

Josephine, "Well they may not be able to tell us where they are hiding, but we could learn how they think and pick up clues from what the children observed and experienced. I especially want to talk to the seventeen-year-old girl that escaped. I think she will definitely be a big help."

They headed to the hotel and settled in while Josephine headed to the police department to speak with the detectives. They welcomed her and gave her a breakdown of the rules. Anything she discovers is to be shared with them immediately. They warned her that there as a fine line between helping and interfering, so they wanted her to be clear and safe.

Josephine, "Not a problem, I'm here to help in whatever way I can to bring these monsters to justice."

They gave her some files, so she could look them over before they meet tomorrow.

She went back to the room. Josephine, Ogard, and Leskha started digging through the files while Amalia researched the information.

When Josephine came across the pages that detailed the ordeal these kids went through, she had a kaleidoscope of emotions running through her body. The victims were severely underdeveloped because of the lack of nutrition and sunlight. They had thick scars around their wrists and ankles from the shackles. Scars all over their bodies, missing teeth, patches of missing hair. The medical records showed the older females had multiple miscarriages. The boys were also sexually assaulted. Broken bones that healed and were broken again. And this is just the physical injuries that we can see. The children's ages range from two to twenty-nine-years-old.

Amalia uncovered that Louise was into dark arts and that her and David were actually part of a cult. That could mean that maybe the cult is harboring them to avoid prosecution.

Josephine, "When I get to the police department in the morning, I'll find out if they had any type of computer that we could take a look at. If they do, there has to be something on there regarding this cult. Unless they are totally off the grid. In which case we will have to go undercover to find them and infiltrate the cult."

The Kurkin's didn't have a computer, but it turned out that there are underground clubs for recruiting couples into the cult. The detective on the case and Josephine discussed an undercover operation. We decided to send Ogard and Leskha in as a couple. But we need to mentally prepare them and rough them up a little, so they look the part.

Ogard, Leskha, and Amalia headed to the station to work with the detectives on the cover story.

Detective, "We need to be sure they are completely believable. These people are dangerous. They have no problem hurting innocent children for pleasure. Imagine what they could do to adults that are betraying them. Well…Let's make sure we don't find out."

While Ogard and Leskha worked, the detectives, Amalia, and Josephine researched the underground clubs. After some digging, we were able to locate two clubs that have "recruiting events."

Leskha and Ogard got ready to head to the club to see if they could get invited inside the group. The place was packed with couples.

Leskha, "Do you think all these people are trying to get in the group?"

Ogard, "God, I hope not, I think the creeps are mixed in with regular folks. Just use the key words so they know we're looking to get in. If they don't respond with any key phrases, we know they are regular people."

Leskha, "This is so disturbing."

Ogard, "Are you sure you're up to this?"

Leskha turned to look at Ogard with such intensity, "I couldn't be more ready to take these freaks down."

They mingled through the club and made their way to the bar. There they noticed a couple was watching them. One of the other couples overheard them using keywords. Ogard sent them drinks with a message for the bartender to deliver. The couple smiled and motioned for us to follow them to a table. We went over and engaged in conversation. After about what felt like an eternity, we left with an invite to come to the club to pledge our way in. Part of the deal was we had to show and describe the abuse we were putting our children through. Though they didn't refer to it as abuse but as pleasure activities conducted on our children.

Once back at the station, Ogard and Leskha briefed the police. Leskha couldn't wait to get back to the room. She felt so dirty and disgusted. While in the shower, Leskha's mind was spinning. She couldn't fathom the thought of a club based on torturing children for pleasure. She prayed for god to give her the strength and focus to complete her mission and take these people down.

Josephine could feel Leskhas's despair. "Are you okay?"

Leskha, "I will be once we bring these people to justice. I'm just distraught, I can't comprehend this, it's making me question the world we live in."

Josephine, "You can't understand because you're good. Don't try to figure them out. Just focus on doing what is necessary to stop them. Think of the victims we save, the pain we will stop."

Leskha, "You're right, I will only focus on the positive outcome."

The next day at the police station, the police provided them with footage and photos of children being abused. They got wired up, dressed, and off we went to meet the couple.

Josephine and Amalia followed closely behind in an SUV with the police. They stopped at a coffee shop and got in the car with the couple to drive to the location. It was a long drive there, on the windy roads to the main path. They arrive at what looks like mountains and dense forest with no paved roads. We had to turn the light off and continue to follow in darkness, so they could not see we were following. The SUV was equipped with a night vision front camera, so that's what we used to get through. The car stopped. They covered the car, so it couldn't be spotted from the road, and continued on foot. After about a half hour, we completely lost signal; we couldn't hear or see them.

Josephine, "I'm going to head in that direction to see if I can get a signal." The police officer told her to stay in the car. Josephine refused and said, "Don't worry, I do this kind of thing all the time. I know how to stay invisible."

She got out of the car before they could stop her and headed down the path. Amalia went with her.

Amailia, "Don't worry, I'll stay out of sight, and if anything goes wrong, I'll run right back to report." Though the police wires and camera failed, their equipment worked just fine. It was better this way, so Lenox can remain anonymous.

Police officer one, "I don't know about this; if anything happens to them, we're going to be held responsible."

Police officer two, "Yes, but we are blind and can't communicate back to our command center. I think we need to head in and try to stop whatever could happen."

Police officer one, "I don't want to blow this, this is our chance of finding the Kurkins and taking down this group. I'll stay here and get closer in case anything happens. Head down the road, stop as soon as you get a signal and request back up."

Ogard and Leskha enter the club. They were blind folded and walked into a room. They took the blind folds off to see that they sat across a table from what appeared to be two women in masks. One was white and the other black or Latino by the color of their hands.

The white one, "I'm Nancy, and this is Maxine, our apologies for the blind folds, but we can't risk exposing our members without being sure that you two are legit and serious about becoming part of us."

Maxine, "You were asked to bring photos and videos of the pleasure acts you've committed, do you have that with you?"

Leskha, "Of course," she reaches into her bag and pulls out a folder with photos and a usb drive.

Maxine takes it, "Give us a few minutes to review, we'll be right back."

The two of them head into another room. The couple from the bar told them they needed to be sure. Can't let just anyone in.

Ogard, "Not a problem, we would do the same."

Leskha, "Do you have a restroom?"

Leskha went into the restroom and locked the door. There was a vent above the hand dryer. She used her rope claw to climb up and look inside. She could see light, so she climbed in and crawled through to peek in the other room. She couldn't believe what she was seeing.

She recognized a few faces. News castors, politicians, celebrities. She took some quick photos, placed a camera, and messaged Amalia and quickly returned to the restroom before she raised suspicions. She re-entered the room to join Ogard while they waited for Nancy and Maxine to return with their answer.

Meanwhile Amalia received the message and was able to tap into the camera to find a way in undetected. She was able to break through their firewalls and tap into the the security system and cameras. Things were coming along better than we planned. We have eyes and a way in. Now we just need to locate the Kurkins, isolate them from the group, and bring down this child torture group.

We quickly scanned the the cameras and found the Kurkins hiding out in the bedroom on the east wing of the third level. Lenox crawled through the vents at lightning speed. She dropped through the ceiling, and Mr. Kurkin took a swing at her. She stopped his fist and squeezed his hand, crushing it, the sound of his bones snapping and crunching, he fell to his knees. Mrs. Kurkin grabbed a chair and swung at Lenox from behind. Lenox turned with a round kick and kicked the chair out of her hands, causing Kurkin to lose her balance and falling. Lenox looked at her eyes. She just wanted to knock the shit out of her, smack that stupid look off her face. Kurkin got up and lunged at Lenox. Lenox put her hand up, and Kurkin started to convulse; quickly she turned to Mr. Kurkin. He went for his gun, she pressed one of her rings on her band and then a laser, knocking the gun out of his hand. He started backing up against the wall, cowering in fear. What a pathetic excuse for a man. Not so tough now since I'm not tied up, starved, and weak for you to torture. Coward. She resisted her urge to kick his face in and put him in a catatonic state. The two of them convulsed in pain.

Mr. Kurkin was feeling himself being sodomized with broom sticks, being whipped, feeling his flesh ripping off with every lashing. He felt his bones breaking from kicks to the ribs and punches to the head while tied up, unable to run. Mrs. Kurkin was experiencing starvation, followed by violent vomiting. Her hair being ripped out at the root with skin coming with it and her face being bitten. A chunk of her cheek flapping. Bruises all over her body. They both just laid there, in their pathetic existence reliving the pain they inflicted. This kind of evil will endure unending pain and fear, emotionally, physically, and metantally.

Meanwhile at the shelter, the kids were experiencing a sense of euphoria, a calm came over them. The fear and pain was leaving their bodies. Bones were healing, their spirit lifting. Though their memories of what they endured were still there. It was somehow bearable, they didn't feel afraid anymore. They felt strength and appreciation for life. Appreciation for being together and a zest for life.

Lenox left the Kurkins on the floor agonizing in the living hell of their own creation and ran into the main hall to capture the remainder of the group.

Maxine and Nancy came out to speak to Ogard and Leskha when they heard the commotion.

They turned to Ogard and Leskha and said, "You did this!" Maxine lunged at Leskha. Leskha moved to the side, grabbed her face, and dropped her to the floor.

She then punched her in the face, screaming, "You sick bitch, I'm going to make you pay." Ogard grabbed Nancy and put her in a sleeper hold, causing her to drop her gun and fall to the floor.

Leskha tied up Maxine; the other couple that brought them there were so scared, they just ran out of the room. Dammit! Leskha shouted as she ran after them. Ogard went after Leskha to help since she ran into the main room that was full of cult members. Unaware that Lenox was already in there and had them convulsing. Lenox turns and sees a couple trying to run. She took out her crossbow and shot them with tranquilizers. They turned, looking up at Lenox; the husband was so scared, he soiled his pants.

Lenox: "Really? You're more of a loser than I thought."

He cowered in a ball, begging Lenox not to hurt him. Lenox, "So I should show mercy the way you showed the children you abused!? She got so angry when she put her hand up to put him in the catatonic state, he went flying across the room, hitting a table, breaking it, there he was, laying on his back, whimpering in fear. She stood over him, all seven-foot-four of her amazonian glory and unleashed. He began to feel everything he's done. She turned to the wife that Orgard was holding. Leskha ran up and open hand slapped her across the face so hard, her hand throbbed.

"Easy, Leskha, I got this." Lenox just had to look at her and she went to her knees in pain convulsing.

Ogard, "We have to go back and get the ring leaders, Nancy and Maxine." They ran back to find they had escaped.

Leskha, "Crap!"

Amalia messaged Lenox, "Get out of there, the police are here with SWAT. They're going in!"

Leskha, "The bathroom is right there, the vent is above the hand dryer." Lenox took off and went through the vent. She emerged on the outside through the vent as Josephine to find Amalia out there talking to the police.

Josephine, "I got a glimpse of what's going on in there." She explained she saw a lot of couples and what room the Kurkins were in. Leskha and Ogard are still in there.

Ogard and Leskha tied each other up and gagged themselves in the back room to throw off suspicion.

Police, "You two stay here, we're going in."

The police headed in with a SWAT team. They split up to cover more ground. The two detectives on the Kurkins case headed right to where Josephine said they were. There they were lying on the ground convulsing, murmuring nonsense. As they scanned the room, they see signs of a struggle, chair turned over, picture off the wall, broken lamp.

Detective one, "What's wrong with them?"

Detective two, "They're probably on some drugs and got into some kind of argument. Who cares, just cuff them up and throw them in the paddy wagon. Finally bring these bastards to justice."

SWAT surrounded the lounge where all the couples were gathered and told them to get on the floor, one by one they each got cuffed.

Josephine to Amalia, "I wish we had more time, I didn't get a chance to punish the rest of the couples, and two got away."

Amalia, "I'll track them down, then you can bring them to justice. They can't hide for long. You did what we came here for. To get the Kurkins, and we took down a child torture ring as a result. It's a win, a good day. And we can't let them know Lenox exists."

Josephine, "I know, you're right. I just want to fix everything."

As the police paraded the perps out of the building, we couldn't believe it. People you'd least expect. Politicians, world renowned doctors, professors. Judges were amongst the group.

Knots built up in Josephine's stomach. These are influential people we are supposed to trust. That are supposed to help mold society. Healers and lawmakers. Though we did a good thing, it was difficult to feel good about it when you see how deep the infectious evil has spread.

Amalia, "Are you okay?, come on, today we won."

Josephine, "I know, I would feel better if we got the ring leaders. I need to talk to Ogard. We need to recruit help in our missions."

They brought out the Kurkins and placed them in a separate police car to bring them back to holding cells. The police detectives thanked Josephine and Amalia for their help.

Police, "We also found your friends; they were tied up and gagged but otherwise unharmed. We are taking them to medical to be looked over, but they look fine."

They got back into the SUV and headed back to the police headquarters to debrief and wait for Ogard and Leskha to rejoin them.

When they got back to the station, Josephine asked if it was possible to see the children before she left. They said they would double check with the psychologist, but they didn't think that would be a problem.

The next morning before they left, they headed over to meet the children. Josephine met with the social worker prior to entering. She said she's seeing a major improvement. They seem to have gotten better overnight. Not sure what changed, but I'm happy for their progress. This made Josephine feel good. When she entered the room, they greeted her with smiles. Their ages ranged from two to twenty-nine. They each seemed to be taking on a role in their family. The caretaker, the protector, the comic. They were full of life and joy. So grateful to have this second chance at life. To have survived and come out stronger on the other side. They were rejoicing, now knowing that their parents were caught and would never be able to hurt another child. This brought a sense of peace to Josephine. She could see the light now, this gave her more strength to deal with her purpose. She told the kids when they were healed that they are welcome to come to the sanctuary, all expenses paid. To learn about the animals and help care for them. They loved the idea.

With that Josephine left. Ogard, Leskha, and Amalia were waiting outside for her. They had to make one more stop to talk to the detectives before heading to the airport.

Detective, "We just wanted to thank you for all your help. You not only helped us capture the Kurkins, but we were able to disassemble a child torture ring. With the information we're gathering from the perps in custody, we are confident that Maxine and Nancy will also soon be captured. We hope you got enough material for your story, and thank you again. Your help will always be welcomed here."

They were about to leave when they saw breaking news. Kim Jung was threatening the US with nuclear bombs. They went one to speak of the horrific things this tyrant was doing to his own people and the evil way he came into power.

Josephine, "You have to be kidding me," shaking her head.

It's like the world is in chaos. Leskha, Ogard, and Amalia all looked at each other. We knew where we were off to next.

They thanked the police for their time and allowing them to assist. With that they headed to the airport. Amalia started giving further into the reports on Kim Jung.

"When we get back home, we'll come up with a game plan on how to stop this mad man."

Josephine to Ogard, "Can you get in touch with others you have mentored? We're going to need a bigger team if we are going to succeed in restoring the balance between good and evil. Evil is one upping us, can't have that."

Leskha, "Hell no, girl…"

We laughed, have to keep your sense of humor. They got on the flight and headed back to Florida.